I0761946

RED MAGIC

Red Magic

I'm in the market for you still.
I *always* will be, sweet bird.

1

A day is but a small eternity, for what is the rising of the sun if not the beginning? What is the setting of it if not the end of life itself? Our sleep is a short, sweet death from which we rise like phoenixes, and this is how I promise to be with you always. Love, I will come back stronger every day to show you how the sky was formed, how it was then trapped within your eyes to now have complete and utter control over me. This will be the morning, when I rise with the intensity of a thousand stars to show you I am but a small fragment of what resides within you, for you are so incredibly grand.

Love, I will then show you how the sea was formed, how it dances with the moon and how its waves are a reminder of their perfect rhythm with each other. This will be the night. This will be us, when I set slowly but surely like a feather upon your skin. I will find my way in the dark, brushing and exploring, searching for the meaning of tomorrow along your lips, searching for how it will taste to love you even more after my rebirth.

If there was ever doubt, my love, understand now that I have forever been in love with the cycles of the sun and the phases of the moon, that I admire the changes of the seasons for every unique speck of life they bring to me. It is the same with you. A day is a small eternity, and I will learn to fall in love anew with every passing lifetime, for every version of you is a version I cannot live without. So, darling, what is the rising of the sun if not your waking eyes? What is the setting of the sun if not our love made beneath the moon?

2

Which road do you walk upon, darling? You, with orchids and lilies and petals of every other kind wrapped around your skin like Nature's very own tribute to you, the vines rising from the earth and lacing you like anklets, claiming every step you place upon the ground as you run free of everything else that does not belong. You, with a heart of red rose and kisses that reach past the flesh, that seep and sink into the depths of my blood and soul.

What words do you whisper when you blossom like spring, the sentences drifting, lingering and reaching my ears so softly?

Oh, how it sounds, this language I can barely understand, the essence of your breath and life scented like a garden in the wind. Rustle and entwine our limbs like stems entangled beneath the sun, and let us speak like this. Let us brave the grasping of each other tightly like roots reaching and holding far below, embracing the piercing parts of our nature, accepting the price of thorns because the beauty ... the beauty is worth it all.

3

The heavens cracked, its stars exploding into shards of light. They shot through the clouds, dancing wildly, drunk and full of fire. The end of the world was the birth of you, the start of life beneath the spectacle. Constellations were painted upon your skin, and I, my love, became an astronomer.

You were candlelight, the incandescence of phoenix fire. You were rebirth, a dream pulled from the darkness of a midnight sleep. You were here, warmth while I was buried in the snow. You were sweet. You were love. You were perfect.

Darling, you were clarity after awakening.

4

You tied infinity to a thread, the endless cycle of our souls' rest and awakening, and you gently tied the knots around me. You weaved the strings, aligned the stars accordingly to finally shed light on this fragment of time. We had always been here, love, paused patiently in this eternity, simply waiting for the right time, for the right moment to begin this perfect show.

5

We gave thanks years ago for the stars that collided, that crashed and burned and lit the pyres on the sacred grounds that connected our heartstrings. We let the flames from the skies illuminate the way a thousand times, and a thousand times we gave thanks. We stepped throughout the years, throughout the sands of time as they tried to swallow us. We stared at the giants, the trials, as we sunk slowly.

"You will NOT defeat us!" we screamed.

"You will NOT!" we yelled viciously, proudly.

And we bottled each other deeply into our souls like messages sent out to sea, treasure maps waiting to be found again by the perfect mixture of chance, patience, and something far greater than fate.

I gave thanks for the ways we came, the ways we disappeared, the lessons in how to love like every day was our last. And then I gave thanks for my last day, for I already knew that from this dust we had become we would be born again. Yet, this time greater. This time brighter.

6

The structure of time broke, the stars listening to our jazz, watching patiently, quietly as the ripples of one dimension fell into another. What wisdom belonged to those lights, to their infinite and uninterrupted shining? What power did they have at that specific moment, during the blinking of my eyes, the fluttering of your breath close to me, the gentle steps guided by song, the fingers grasping, holding tightly to the fabric of my clothes, to the fabric of that very second itself?

I fell through the gap, darling, after living an entire life on my own, and here I am again. Would you believe me if I were to tell it to you now, here, as we dance once more, as both our hearts find the perfect rhythm to beat to? We have been here before, darling. Do you believe me? Is this how second chances are made?

I saw us painted on the walls, mosaic glass shifting, legs and arms entwining, mixing like colors from two worlds apart. I saw our story etched, carved in marble like old myths. We were written before we knew, destined to be found, love, to be lost only ever within each other.

7

May we journey in our sleep and venture out to sea like ships in search of treasures. May we find them, every single one, and come to realize in these dreams it was each other we had been searching for all along. May you use the stars to reach me, love, for I am already making my way to you. May the winds help you sail faster. May they whisper the three words I've always felt for you.

8

The sea was desperate to keep us apart, but how little did it know of wings, of how they constructed themselves from thin air to later be placed upon our backs, sewn perfectly along our skin, and giving us finally the choice to fly. The sea tried desperately to live between our spaces, to misguide our paths with violent waves until one day it realized we soared high above it, that we, in all our glory, glided beneath the sun.

To find a way to you has always been my way of life; to learn to do the impossible, a skill everyone else has given up on. I will not let the depths swallow us, my love, for even if one day our wings find themselves tired and unable to fly, I will catch the both of us atop the shifting blue. I have learned to swim for moments like these, for when you desperately need these hands to calm you, for when you, darling, feel the need to grab hold and float on top of me.

We will always find a way, love.

I promise we will always find a way.

9

What fear was left within the earth, and what did it matter? You and I are of the sky, my love, birds soaring swiftly through the clouds, stopping to rest only in the sea, only as we turn into dragons of the deep. What fear was left within the mountains, darling, and why would we ever care?

We are made of something else, of particles unfamiliar to this world. Can you not see as feathers turn into scales, as we learn to fly and swim together? What else could matter when we love like this, when we've learned to live so free?

10

What curious animals we were, you and I. What curious animals we still are. How did we find comfort throughout the years, sanity, after all this time shielding, keeping with no logical reasoning our wondering at bay? Will we live through the instinct? Will our bodies survive the fury, the fiery relief of our souls when they finally meet, when the red strings of their fates finally knot into what has always been meant to be?

These notes I leave for you, my love, these secret messages encoded with your name. These are the things I leave behind, the fragments of my voice, the chance for you to hear me even as I sleep. This is the trail I've left, the crumbs for you to follow. These are dotted lines, my wanderer, marks along all the treasure maps I've sent to you. They'll lead you here, I promise, to all the X's I've plotted along my skin. I am waiting, and soon I'll wake. So, be here when I do.

Be here, my love. I have missed you.

11

I held my hand out to the sky, my fingers reaching for the lights that resembled the freckles upon your cheeks. Did you know, love, that there is a sea above us too, that all those brightly lit stars are like grains of sand glimmering as we finally reach the shore? I held my hand out in an attempt to swim, to fly, to somehow find my way to you. You are in all things, love.

You are always here.

12

You were the storm and I was the sea. Your lightning crashed upon me, but I survived, my waves violently racing across the shores, desperately trying to find the mountains. How can I reach higher from these tides? How can I, my love, soften thunder into laughs?

Tell me, and I will do the impossible.

13

I unraveled within your sea, forfeiting my title as captain, surrendering to the depth of your oceans. I was lost here once, ages ago, but somehow I found land. I realize now I was always meant to be lost, to be tangled within the fiery essence of your setting suns, your shifting sands, and the fury of your waves. I realize now, more than anything, I have always, truly, belonged to the sea.

14

I dreamt of ocean waves, the gentle echoes of their breaking. You were the distant light across the sea, the star guiding me back to shore. My eyes never lost sight of you. I stayed, patiently navigating, watching as you intricately cut through the fog. I'm grateful everyone else searched for the moon while I instead searched for you, for, darling, you were so much brighter, so much more beautiful. You were my wonder, love, a secret I did not want to share.

15

We were ashes scattered in the wind, spread across the ocean by chance. Would the shore bring us together once more? Would the waves carry us?

What lies beyond the smoke, the smog, the fumes of all our living souls? What is hidden out there between us all? What is waiting there for you and me?

Come here, darling, finally, gently, and stir with me like warm morning coffee. These mornings ache for you. These arms, they beg for you.

16

Flames were tossed into the empty spaces. They stirred and danced until the flares became the gentle curls of your hair. Stars were thrown into the mix too, and those became the untamable glimmer of your eyes, the light within each of your sapphire skies. Whose hand was responsible for creating you this way, for intricately crafting your birthmarks like seashells scattered across the ocean floor? Who fashioned your lips from rose petals and concocted your mouth to taste like sweet, addictive honey?

Tell me, for I'm dying to know of this magic, of this undefined and secret science that watered the seed for you to grow. Tell me, love, for there is so much more of you I have yet to learn.

Rock me unsteady, please, with the burning touch of skin on skin, of lips on lips. Pull me apart, breath by breath. Make me anew.

Behind every great man is the story of an even greater woman, one who made him far better than he could have ever been on his own.

17

Was it selfish of this universe to create you the way it did, to pluck stars from the heavens and gently place them in your eyes, to bathe you in fire and color your hair as the setting sun? Was it selfish to spend it all on you, to give you every perfect piece scattered amongst the eternal cosmos, to mix it all, and have you born into the beautiful collection of light that you now are? And was it selfish of me, my bird, to steal you away when the universe was done, to love you so deeply, to feel, darling, as I do now?

18

The world knew of seven seas, my love, and only those have they ever tried to navigate. I discovered more, two coupled oceans contained by magic, by a force that does not follow any laws of physics. I ventured down the valley of your back once, and I returned, retracing kisses to your neck. Do you remember, darling?

You rolled over to meet your lips with mine, and it was then that I witnessed the crashing of secret waves. There was a faint glimmer of lighthouses hidden in your eyes, and it was then that I saw the blue, the shining of the endless depths. The world knew of seven seas, my love, but I'm so glad that I discovered two. Those are mine and mine alone. I will sail within them, infinitely.

I promise.

19

Every day I discover a secret to your creation. I waited patiently in the water, love, and watched the sun sink into the ocean today. The orange eclipsed beneath the waves, and when it dimmed, I realized the resting star was a mirror to your pupils. Fire lashed out once more, just before the darkening, just before the night claimed the sky. The streaks of red were the passion built within your eyes, the divine lights that hide within the sea of your precious irises.

20

We were stones lost in the skipping, in the tossing of fate's little game. Little did they know we planned it all. Little did the universe imagine how we chose to sink together, to be left deep in the waters of our own darkness. We chose the abyss because we did not need to see. We chose the darkness because we felt it all. That was always more than enough.

21

I've slow-danced once and only once. I've stepped on stars and clouds and swayed to the sound of jazz lost in the wind, comet tails dusting my skin with magic light, only once. Once was nice. Once was good.

Twice would be to dance on the sun, to tiptoe and glide on flames and learn to burn brighter than any star lit among us. Twice would be to die in the fire, to be reborn as one and learn to plummet down to Earth, the light itself chasing us as we become the very thing every lover learns to wish upon.

22

We sank beneath the submarines, the water pushing further down, spirals shifting beneath the sea. We were caught in the twisting, in the plummeting. Will they see us, darling? Will the world understand how even here there is love? Even in the silence. Even in the dark.

23

I do not know, love, how stars became synonymous with eyes, how their dust became birthmarks upon your skin. I do not know, so tell me how skies and seas hide within you, how this whole world becomes so minuscule when it stands beside you.

How grand you must be, my sweet bird, to hold the constellations as an audience within your thoughts, to defy the laws of this universe and have magic bloom from your very fingertips. I do not know what you have done, what you will continue to do, but I am here, darling, endlessly wondering. Here I am, eternally curious.

24

Our blood was young though it carried ancient souls. What bodies we were tossed into, so free, so wild, yearning to learn the things we already carried inside. What spirits we were blessed with, so patient, so wise, willing to relearn and perfect the art of loving each other every time.

Your fury stole the darkness in me and replaced it all with fire, replaced it all with an insatiable hunger for everything you are, everything you've always been.

25

Stars were laced with vines and petals upon your skin, your colors changing like the sky, its setting sun. Flowers bloomed within your lungs, and I hungrily swallowed your every exhale. Something sweeter, my love, I've never tasted. Something grander, my darling, does not exist.

My honesty was spilt in words. Your truth was there in your speechlessness, shed beautifully in tears of joy. I was cleansed as I stood beneath the waterfalls of your eyes, baptized in the truth we spilt, born again in the love we still feel.

Darling, I will swallow their taste as I kiss them all. My love, I promise they will never go to waste.

26

The stars drew near as I told them of you, a legend of one brighter than them, of one whose light purifies the very soul. They raced across the skies to hear my whispers, and I smiled as each one listened, as each one sat in front of me, an audience blinding me with grandeur. If these beautiful creations, my love, are in awe of you, then, truly, how lucky am I to be the one you've chosen?

If they traveled from the heavens to simply hear about you, then a better place than that from which they were born you must be. What else could I ask for if I live in a dimension more beautiful than the birthplace of angels? What else could I ask for, my sweet darling, for I'm so blessed to live in a world with you.

27

I've set fire to bridges to see how long their foundations could last. I've set worlds aflame in search of someone who could burn as bright as I. An arsonist's secret. A longing for more. Then you came and showed what the wait was for.

Breathe, I thought, my lips placed upon your skin.

Breathe, I thought, the world burning still.

She is air.

28

We raced like dragons through time, traveled across the stars in search of brighter lights, and now we've found them, love. We trapped them within our hands, the suns now orbiting around our fingers. What comfort is this now, this gentle breathing of souls, like slow fire burning the cold away within my lungs? You placed your skin upon mine and it was like learning a language all at once, like learning to inhale the ether properly, like discovering once more what it's like to drink sweet nectar.

We raced like dragons, love, exploding through the chaos like fireworks, our spirits dancing as our bodies shook, as they glowed in ecstasy. What beauty is this, darling? How have you taught me to see as if for the first time, to taste as if lips had never met mine? How is it that everything with you is new? How is this possible, my bird, when our love is as ancient as the moon?

29

We tumbled into the sea, salt mixing into waves and foam. We fell deeply together, plunged far into the infinite abyss to find that, though the vast ocean would thrash our particles violently, we would always find a way. We sunk to the bottom, to where the world stood still, and we held hands as we looked high above toward the faint glimmers of light.

We pushed. We jumped and flew, glowing once more. We carried each other, deciding to start once more. And we smiled, love, knowing this would be the last and perfect time.

30

What do we call the pillars in the dark, the anchors keeping us from drifting away toward the abyss? What do we call the lights, the signs and breaths of fresh air? What do I call completion, love, the final piece adjusted perfectly to fit into this fragmented heart? What do I call a life? What do I call a home?

Darling, of all those things, what do I call you?

31

My body broke beneath the waves, the crashing of the ocean's fury set upon me, yet I held the sky still, arms outstretched, balancing the heavens on my back as stars collided into my spine. I will endure it all, every bit of it, for you, my love, for if there is ever any doubt, it is here in my steadiness, in my determination that you will find the answers. I would sooner die to keep this weight off you than ever give up. I would do so with a smile. I would do so happily, darling, for you are my key to living. You, and only you, are like breathing.

32

If there is romance in suffering, in the agony of existence and the darkness, then I am not a romantic man. You have taken all of that away. You have brought nothing but joy.

33

You tossed and turned in the night, and my fingers didn't need the light to know how to find you. They knew you flawlessly, where to find your gentle spine like a magnet in the dark, what specific steps to climb to travel lightly across your back, what edges to soften to guide you home, to guide you to your peace. I will wake as you do, darling, for my soul is just as restless as yours. It's desperately eager, I'd say, to love whenever it can, to find any excuse to hold you, to let you know it belongs to you.

Only you.

34

I heard you in the distance, past the clouds and the infinite waters. I burned for you even in my silence. Can you see the glow? Have you found it, love?

You are the rarest form of flower, a constant fire that blooms into stars, your petals like comets when they fall, racing furiously across the skies. You are not of this earth, love. Your roots are somewhere else, somewhere much more beautiful.

And how to find that dimension? I thought. Home was a place I longed for without knowing where it was. Then I walked into your forest and I learned the truth.

Home, darling, was you.

35

Home was hidden between the leaves, a shelter beneath the shade. I stood over you, arms wrapped around your soul, shielding your life as the fire etched its mark upon my back. The stars threw their fury at us, love. They launched their flames, but none of them ever burned you.

Home was constructed within the bark, within the hardened flesh that allowed you to remain gentle inside. I was an ancient thing, a creature designed for resilience, for hope, despite all the storms. I will be here, love, as permanent as the sky, even when you forget. My roots will never let you crumble. My branches will never let you fall.

36

Oh, how you've found your way, darling. How you've crawled atop of me, so gently, so softly. What did you find here, lost in curiosity, when your hands navigated like your soul? What was there beneath the skin, beneath the armor only you have managed to seep through, love? Tell me of those secret things, the melted gold between your fingers, the treasures you, and only you, have discovered.

You were born to wander, to be drawn to the mysterious nature of these lights. So, how do I show you, my sweet bird, that there are suns buried deep within me, troves of words that will live only to describe and explain the beautiful rarity of all you've ever been to me? Tell me, how far did you reach? How resilient were your fists as they dug beneath the bone?

Oh, how patient you were to etch this path inside me, to carve and chisel away with laughter the stone that hid the hollow. Come, darling, for no one else deserves the space you have created. Lie inside this cradle, this warm nest you have constructed where my heart once was. Have you not yet realized that the light was always you, that I now shine because it is here where you have chosen to rest?

37

The skies could not understand how I repeatedly stole their clouds, how I brought them down to gift you shade, to give you rest when exhaustion crept into your bones. The sun could not comprehend how, even in its light, I found the right amount of rain to water you, to quench your thirst when your petals needed to bloom.

Have you understood this yet, my love, that I will move the mountains and I will still the seas for you? Have you realized all that I will do for you?

38

I felt the humming like rumbling thunder, the blood rushing, vibrating as we journeyed through the night. The fiery tips of my fingers fell upon your skin, planting flags of lightning along each valley conquered, along each curve and edge discovered. They sent electricity deep into the center of you, of your primal, caged self.

This is our process, my bird. I will bend the bars until they break, the metal that's kept you trapped away from what you've always needed. I'll send fury, my love, like an Olympian god, and break the chains the world has set upon you.

Darling, you will be free. You will stay wild.

39

And if one day, my love, the clouds all fell upon this earth like mighty snow, know that I would never yield. I would stand my ground, arms stretched out to the heavens like pillars toward the sky, screaming, "I will not let you harm her."

Know, my darling, that I have endured far worse than the splitting of the blue, the cracking of the space we see above us. I'll place the stars within my hands to keep you warm. I'll endure the burning of my flesh, for the scars that will form will be the permanent reminders of what this heart of mine feels for you every single day. This world would be a littler place without you. This world, my love, would not be as grand.

40

Love, how would this world be if it was moved as you move me? How much more beautiful would this life be if they were all inspired the way you inspire me, the way you feed beauty into my thoughts, transform it into words, to then paint a picture of you, of love, of eternity with symbols and characters we've come to understand as a language?

Where could this take our souls, all seven billion, if they could learn to communicate the way I do with you? Would it be so difficult, my darling, to love so fiercely and be adored in return, to be loved like air itself? Do you think the world will ever understand the necessity of you and me, the example amongst the crowd of the impossible finally come to be, of perseverance, of patience, and sweet addiction?

Love, tell me if you know, for I've seen visions of the future in your eyes, how would this world move if it danced like us, if it properly learned to push and pull in balance like the ocean waves? Tell me, love, how holy could this world be? How in touch with the heavens could we become?

41

Our fingers wrapped around each other's like knots, the red strings of our souls blooming from our hands like vines, weaving slowly together in a holy entwine of two mystic creatures. I felt the curves, the lines etched across your skin, as if I was born to be the sole reader of your palms. How this world created you to fit so perfectly into me is beyond any human knowledge. How this universe constructed our paths so intricately in its web is a secret kept only by God. How do I explain that I can feel when in your veins your blood pumps through? How do I explain, darling, that your love is mine too?

We were light split at birth, the dust of a single star that blew in separate directions. Bone and flesh grew upon our particles, molded uniquely by the different winds that carried us apart, but we, love, are a single soul. These ribs inside feel just as yours do. These lungs breathe the same air you breathe. Can you not see that we are familiar because I am as much of you as you are of me, that our essence is one, that we are simply trying to be complete?

42

What magic is there in the combination of two, in the futures to be born with fire laced within their hair, with fragments of your seas and skies within their eyes and constellations spread beautifully across their skin? There is a heart-shaped birthmark where only you know exists, and they will have it too, a reminder that all our hearts are linked to yours as mine forever will be.

What magic is there in the endless combinations to discover, in the trees to climb together and the playful laughter to be heard? Will they have feet that dance like mine and hands that heal like yours, the passionate and wild curiosity of us both? What beauty lies within that journey, love? Will they learn to breathe as you and I, the patience inhaled within our lungs, and kindness exhaled out to the world?

Oh, what magic they will be. Oh, what wonders to be found...

43

How did the clouds fashion the curves of your legs, love, the gentle surface that rises and falls as you pull me in closer? How did the stars fall so precisely upon your skin? How powerful must you be, darling, to withstand the fury of all those lights, the comets and their dust, and still be here, so beautiful, so kind? How did the winds mold you into all you are? How were you constructed to be so gentle, so fierce and free all at the same time?

Clouds became steppingstones as you gently walked upon them, the settling fog becoming the last step for you to reach this earth. How did you learn, love, to move the way you do, to dance and stir and bend as if the wind itself was injected into your veins?

Oh, water became a surface for you to stand upon, so can you see now, my darling, the reflections of fire? Have you understood yet the yearning I feel, the desperation to touch the rolling of hips and the swaying of your soul? What thunder lives within your belly. What longing I have to feel your electricity.

44

What else was left to say when words had already come running out, had already spilled across our skin like fire dancing in the woods before we could actually speak them? What syllables were shared by silent lips, by their touch instead of the sound of the shapes our voices formed? How is it, love, that we learned to speak in the rustling of our sheets, in the entwining of our bodies? What magic is this, darling? How is it that we learned to understand when not a single word was spoken? And tell me, love, how all this longing translated into our silent "I love you."

I craved the salt of your skin, to taste your oceans entirely, not a piece left unconquered by my lips. I craved the essence of your soul, the ethereal particles that slipped beautifully through your pores.

45

What strange obsession with the sea, to plunge into its depths time and again, each time reaching deeper, further, each time curious for more. What incomprehensible addiction this is, love, to rise as I run out of breath, to surge with the foam and the salt and gasp for oxygen, to know and understand that each time I feel more and more alive.

How far do they go, my darling, those eyes, that soul, for I have yet to reach their ends? How do you contain the storms, the winds, all the violent waves? What strength lies even deeper than the sapphire, than the ocean that rages on?

How fearful they must have all been, my love, everyone before me, not to understand that clouds and thunder are nothing more than passion bursting from within, that the splitting of the heavens, the lightning cracking like a whip; they are all just as much a part of you as the stillness, just as much a part of you as the calm.

46

I must have swallowed you in a dream, for I awoke with a familiar taste in a foreign place. I must have found you as we slept, etched a path throughout the nightly realms, and devoured you completely in our dreams. The air still smells like you, love.

Your name still sweet as it rolls off my tongue.

47

How jealous I grow of this air, its privilege to know the warmth within your lungs, to come out, be released as a sweet and long exhale in your lazy mornings. How jealous I am of the sun, its undeserving right to gently fall upon your skin with its light. What must I do to be that close, my love, to you? How do I transform myself into the taste inside your mouth, the blood within your veins, the dreams you catch as I remain here restless and awake? How do I reach you when you sleep? What can I do to be that close to you?

48

What magic you fed me, love. What potion you let drip past my lips, the liquid addiction to all you are. I slept enslaved to you, a prisoner to your touch, the lingering feeling that dances on my flesh even when you're not here. What sweet cage this is, this place within your ribcage. Why, my darling, would I ever want to escape this lovely fortress? Leaving, for me, from the start, was never an option.

49

What chemicals did you birth inside my head? What combination, love, of science and magic have you practiced to cause this kind of hunger, this kind of longing? How did you melt into my mouth and find your way down my throat, nectar swallowed in the form of you, of your soul, and then manage to diffuse slowly into my bloodstream? Do you realize, darling, that if I bleed, it is you that comes spilling from within? Do you know that it is you I breathe, that it is you my heart unfailingly pumps?

50

Eyes shut. Soul drifting. There is grace here. There is peace in the dream, in the second chances found. I am burning, love, with every kiss. Your lips dance like fire upon my skin, and it is in this heat, this warmth, that I wish to stay.

Eyes still shut. The hint of a faint smile spreading. I found you there, darling, hidden in my sleep, hidden in the dark. This is our secret place.

51

Morning light spiraled into my sleep, claiming my dreams gently with its fire. I awoke between the foam, between the gentle rustling of sheets. My body healed atop the waves within this cradle, more and more as the soft rumbling of another soul slowly drifting toward me grew stronger.

I awoke to the warmth of a sweet bird landing upon me. I, her only haven, the one she always chose throughout this vast ocean to find a respite, to rest her gentle wings. I awoke to two blue skies, to the beautiful sound of salvation.

52

Your hands came to me like gifts from God, the weaving of their fingers through my hair, searching for the answers to all your hidden questions. Can they read my thoughts, love, as they sift gently through this heavy mind? Do they understand, those soft and nimble things, that I am here to stay? Do they comprehend, darling, that I am deeply interwoven with your soul? Do they know that you, and only you, are home?

53

Wake with me and let this breathing rise like smoke. It is art what we've become, what you have done, love, to me. My skin becoming your playground, your canvas, a reminder of the fiery nature of your soul. Wrap around me tighter, darling, and don't be afraid. Dig deeper if you must. I will carry you there.

54

You slowly slipped into another world, eyes first, drifting away towards the blur, towards the haze. Your arms wrapped around my neck, and I, my love, became the anchor to always bring you back. Heavy eyelids were lost in ecstasy. The sounds of our voices became nothing but distant music. Is this what it's like to be free at last? Is this, darling, what it's like to become the love that's made?

55

They shot down from the heavens, a thousand angels in search of music. They didn't know of us, of our laughter mixing in the air. How close were we to surpassing these beings? How close must our human voices have been to come so close to them? They shot down to witness something grand, something much more beautiful than they had ever before seen. They shot down to listen, love, to learn to feel so genuinely, to learn to feel as we do.

56

We grew in the fog, in the unknowing, in the passing of years as we slowly unraveled within each other. Could we not tell before? Could we not feel within the clouds that we had risen side by side, that all we had to do was extend our yearning fingers toward each other and we would find all the answers we had ever searched for? We grew so tall, my love, so grand, and when we finally burst past the darkness, past the blanket of smoke, we finally saw how close we were after all. We then reached even closer to the sun, and its light showed us the branches that were already touching, the roots that spread, entwined with each other, guided by something even more mystical than destiny.

How did we not feel after so much time that our strings were already intricately weaved together, that the same water quenched both our thirsts, and that we were as synchronized as the sea and the movement of its waves? How did we not notice until now, my love, that this heart of mine belongs to you, that yours belongs to me, and that they both beat together beautifully?

57

I've broken mirrors to close all the portals, all the secret tunnels to other dimensions. I've rid myself of all reflections, of every realm parallel to this one. I don't want to chance it, love. There is not a future I would imagine without you, no possibility in any distant universe in which you were not etched permanently into my skin, that you were not stitched closely to the very fibers that hold my being together. There is no other way but us, but here, but you, but me. No other combination exists, no other soul worthy of all the essence I've learned to give. There is no other love but you, darling. Everything, it has always all belonged to you.

58

Each lifetime will amount to a single day in our eternity, love. Each century alive a testament to our souls' unrelenting journey in finding each other time and again. I will write of us with each rebirth, and the world will someday understand. They will find the myths, discover the repeating saga of you and me, hidden throughout the different languages all these versions of myself will have learned, and they will begin to believe in the magical. They will understand, darling, that we have belonged to each other since before our time and that we have continued to love much past theirs.

59

Time will end and I, my love, will still be madly entwined with you. The sun will set one last time, and as we realize it will no longer rise, you will see how we become the light that brings warmth to this darkening earth. The seas will crash and sink into their own depths until everything is gone and dry, and still, my love, I will show you how we become the rain to give life to this world once more. We will love as passionately in the day as we do in the night, and neither time nor the ending of it will decide when I stop loving you.

60

If there is purpose to this love, then it is this. There is patience left if we choose to find it. There is magic if we faithfully choose to believe. If there is purpose to this story, my darling, then it is for something even grander than you and me. We already knew this. We understood we were written before our time. My love, this is all for them, for the world, for the nonbelievers. If there is purpose to this love, then it is simply to witness its existence. It is out there still for all of us to find. It is out there still, if we choose patience, if we choose magic.

61

It was you, my love. Always you. Two souls entwined before time, stuck in endless conversation as the rest of the world passed by. It was you and the essence of all you were even before your birth. You tied me here, our story engraved within the old streets of an old city, and since, my sweet bird, this is where I have been.

Memory has carried me to you every time, and as our souls sit patiently awaiting our return, this body of mine craves you with every minute spent away, with every mile placed in between us. A part of you is still with a part of me, sitting patiently in our chairs, overlooking the sea that rests beyond the walls.

And, love, I know a part of me is still with you, for I purposely chipped away a fragment of myself to secretly place within your hands, to be so close to you in any way or form until the universe is no more. It was you, darling. It was always you that held my heart.

62

We traveled like gypsies, trailing our dancing fingertips along the roads down our bellies. We rolled like rumbling thunder beneath the stars, laughing, crazed, madly in love. How much freer could we have been? What more was there to search for after witnessing this, after living as us?

63

Light was fractured by your touch, the colors streaming and bouncing off your skin. You, a prism designed to scatter the beauty, the warmth. How did you learn to be this way, my love, like glass that shifts in trail of the sun, stained by a thousand hues of water and fire and earth? How were you constructed to be this way, to be so perfectly drawn?

64

Flowers bloomed across your skin, goose bumps painted across the flesh I traveled upon. I trailed your roads, wandering from neck to waist, sliding slowly across the dip and rise of your spine. And what waves you formed, my love, as my lips tickled your ends and you stirred like the wakening sea. How envious must the sun be not to feel the way we feel, so close and free? How envious it must be that we, darling, have finally learned to burn without being consumed by the fire.

How resilient we've grown, to roll as one entwined vine across the flame, to laugh madly in love beneath the skies as we blanket ourselves and hide beneath the dancing embers. What magic is this? What form of transformation, of metamorphosis, have we undergone? Two beasts turned to light. Two stars colliding into a sea of dandelions.

Love, you and I were designed to be as one.

65

A hundred years could pass and the earth would still remember its blooming, its resilience as seeds birth and we, my love, become ghosts. But, darling, not even the end of our time could pull apart the strings, the knots intricately tied to keep our hands, our souls permanently grasped. A thousand years would pass, my sweet bird, but just as the stars shine even after death, so will we. We will be the brilliance, the light found in another place.

66

If time were mapped upon a paper, etched by ink on a mythic piece of white, I would find it and fold it intricately over and over. I would shorten the lines drawn from edge to edge, and I would walk upon the hilltops that would fan out from the creases. What else could I do, darling, to lessen this wait? What secrets are there to unravel? How do I, my sweet bird, learn to fly to see you sooner?

67

Light broke through slowly, warmth trailing up our legs as we awakened. Your freckled skin was golden. Your eyes fluttering open showed me the skies the sun was searching for.

68

You dissipated into the clouds, wisps of smoke dancing in the wind. I will find you again. I will learn to fly. I will breathe you in.

69

There is reward in the patience, in the journey and determination to keep walking, to keep flying towards the light we reach for. There is reward in the unrelenting love, in the chasing of our souls as we trail behind the red strings that connect your heart to mine. I will never tire. I will never quit.

70

Fall here, lips upon skin, feathering the surface in search of something deeper.

Can you taste it, love, the soul brushed onto your tongue, the wisps of the spirit you swallow softly?

71

'Round we go, minutes passing, cycling through days that turn into years. How long have we waited, love? How much of this have we endured? The wheels spinning as we travel, rising and falling and rising again. How resilient we've become, darling. How little we have left of this wait, of this yearning. Our hands will reach soon. Our lips will too.

72

Kisses trailed like wolves racing through the trees, like spirits madly searching for running water. Lips wandered with thirst, with curiosity. Was it the instinct to survive, my love, or was it wonder? What was it that led me to you, to the way you bend, to the way you cleanse this soul of mine?

Tell me, love.

73

What words to describe the surprise, eyes in wonder, in disbelief, of a lingering dream finally coming true? How to compare the faith, something as strong, as unbreakable yet soft and bright and gentle? No other soul will know, will understand, how the rain makes way for us, time simply stopping when you turn towards me, the moon spinning a little faster, dancing and twirling with joy as my arms wrap around you like waves.

You are the world, the earth, the sea, the mountains. And as you reach for the heavens, I am everything in the sky that is so easily pulled to your fingertips by gravity. Embers crackle through my bones when I find you near, and your lips are the finishing spark that set the rest of me aflame. How else, love, do I tell you that every word that slips from our mouths and into the ether around us was designed long before our existence, written and scripted long before our physical births here on this plane?

How else, darling, can I tell you, can I show you that I was born for you, that you were born for me? There is no other way but you, no other path to walk upon than the one that leads to us.

I love you now. I loved you before. I've loved you always. I'll love you forever.

74

I'd spend a thousand years learning the secrets of the universe if it meant spending even only a single minute with you after.

75

We'll slip gently into the fade, into that place in time where dreams overlap reality, the blur, the intertwining of legs as eyes barely open, as smiles curl slowly upon our faces. We'll live in that moment forever, in the satisfaction, the relief, the kisses trailed down a spine that bends as you stretch the sleepiness away. These mornings, love, are all I'll ever need.

76

The game was set, two souls to be knotted eternally, each taking a turn in finding the other, each life to learn of patience, of faith that the one who slept would soon remember too. The game was this, to reawaken the grace, the wonder and curiosity within each other, to remind ourselves that we were written in permanence, in unwavering and undying love. The rules were simple: to never lose, to never stop fighting.

77

Would they understand, my love, if they lived here within our chests, here within the blood that pumps, that runs through the rest of you, through the rest of me? Would they comprehend then, and only then, how deeply buried our souls are within each other, the entwining, the stitching of your name upon my skin, the etching of your words across my bones? Would they be reborn in love, in hope and faith, my sweet bird, if they fell as hard, as madly as you and I?

Would this world learn to breathe more easily, to bloom beneath the light of something new? Oh, love, if only they knew that mountains shift entirely in our direction simply to watch, simply to witness the rare miracle we are. If only they could understand that there is so much more to this than what we see, than what belongs to this specific place in time. What could they all be, what worlds could they conquer if they learned to listen, if they learned to vibrate to the same frequencies as each other? How much more they would gain in the surrendering, in the gentle shutting of the eyes as lips are placed upon the soul.

If only, darling.

If only this world could love like you and I.

78

We were colors tossed into the mix, your lips turning into mine, claws to marks upon skin. We were the painting shifting, alive, as every stroke of the brush pushed and pulled. What relief this is, darling, to be entwined, to be as one, like infinite drops of water in the making of one sea. What beauty this is, our souls grasping tightly, eternally, as two bodies find the answers, as two bodies make love.

79

Dream of this, of here, of now, love. Can you see it? Can you feel it? Dream, and dream of me, the weight of these lips on yours, the dripping of the honey, the swallowing of the nectar.

Oh, how they trace along your skin, the taste of me mixing, melting into the taste of you. Oh, how this soul has faded into yours, not knowing where you end, not knowing where I begin.

80

How deep we run, far below the birds, deeper than the waves, rooted past the earth. Lost, darling, like spirits between the trees. Could they see? Could they understand if they touched like you and I, dripping upon each other's skin like honey ready to be devoured? How mad this love. How beautiful, like flowers blooming from your mouth as my lips plant the seeds, as my tongue finds its way to your own, and the seas learn to part only for us, only for our embrace.

Do you think, my sweet bird, that the earth erupts deep below, that it knows where to lay the sand, where to rise in the vast ocean to form a cradle for us and only us? Do we find rest or do we tumble in our entwinement, skipping like stones across the shallows as beasts that play, as creatures that find innocence in the water? What relief, my love, in the gentle biting. What salvation, darling, in the freedom, in the wild nature of us.

81

Left in longing, in the seconds between our breaths, the fragments of time I am not breathing you in. Warmth. I wish for you as an unending inhale, an eternal scent that somehow always feels new, that somehow always reminds me we're wild, we're free.

You, love, like the sea.

82

If we could be like them, simple yet strong, gentle yet resilient, waves that come and go, crashing against the rocks to soften, to smooth the edges of the jagged. If we could be like them, sinking only to rise, to curl beneath the surface and return with new attempts, never wavering, never ending.

How many times would we learn to push after being pulled, to try again after falling? How many times could we rise beneath the foam, air released from the bubbling only to give life to the souls above the depths? Could they learn too if we showed them our strength? What grace in the acceptance, the balance, the faith. What peace in the knowledge of this, of us, that everything, my bird, has always been meant to be.

If we could be like them, as powerful as the ocean waves, then why not seven billion others as well? Imagine a love so vast it spreads. Imagine us, my darling, a love to change the world.

83

Eyes shutting tightly, wishing, hoping to meet somewhere in the dark. Souls whispering, reaching for fingers that will recognize, that will grab and hold and pull. To dream of you is to have you in a deeper place, to crave you in such a way that I find you in my sleep.

84

The sky split in two for you to simply fall, to finally come crashing down into these longing arms. Oh, how you spun and danced and laughed. You, a miracle on this earth. You, of magic and stardust.

Mesmerized, I got on one knee.

Beautifully, surely, you said, "Yes."

85

Have they seen it yet or would they believe it if we told them? Written in myths. Etched within stars. We've walked among them for the longest time, love. Would they understand it if they witnessed it all, if they lived as long as us? You and I, destined to wander, fated to be hand in hand. Endlessly. Eternally. Would they believe? Would they learn to love like before?

86

We'll measure distance not in miles, not in kilometers. It will be in seconds, in minutes and hours and, at times, even days and months. But, darling, if we measure like this, then every day the distance is smaller, the wait is shorter. We will measure distance not in feet, not in inches, because you are always here. We are never truly far apart. Moments separate our bodies but never our souls. Never our love.

87

Exhaustion that only you and I know, that only you and I could understand. Fall here, love, warmth entwined within apologies, and rest in arms that only want to hold, in a place that will always keep you safe. Exhaustion will come from time to time, but I promise, darling, it will always go just as it arrived. Sleep and dream and know that I am there, that my soul is close, that it blankets you even when we can't touch, even when some days are harder than others.

88

Blooming irises from your eyes, roses from your hair, and sunflowers speckled across your skin. You rose from the sea, from the rustling of sheets, and swam across with no fear. You, a garden on a moving island, reaching for me, lazily smiling, stretching with a gentle moan of relief.

"Good morning, darling."

I pulled you in.

89

Oh, love, how I'll carry you forever, hands wrapped around, legs entwined, and me, darling, feeling your warmth against me. I'll split the seas to walk through them, to show you the mysteries of the ocean floor as I walk you to the other side of the world. How much I will learn as I hold you like this, your whispers and laughs close to my ear, your secrets and dreams dripping like honey into my thoughts.

Smile, darling, and I will too. My joy is here caught between my hands, held tightly as a treasure. My happiness, love, is the way you look as you gaze into the distance, as you stare with certainty that it is us, that it has always been us, that we from the beginning of time have been meant to be. My happiness is the awe, the wonder, as I feel the soul pouring from your lips, rising past your skin.

My happiness, sweet bird, is you.

90

Winds will blow long past our time, for thousands of years and long past our bodies turning to dust. Winds will blow, disperse us across the sea. But we won't be gone. We will be carried. Our story will become whispers to those who listen to the rustling of the leaves, to those who listen to the crashing of the waves.

91

Love wrapped in exhales, the rising of air, the release from lungs filled with music, song bubbling to the surface like flags held high after conquest. Rain falling as the pressure is dispersed, drops streaming, carving trails of joy, marks on cheeks like footprints from the dancing, the wild and graceful nature of our spirits.

92

Realize how we've always come back to each other, two souls wandering, exploring and learning in order to come back here to this familiar place. We wake and live and drive out to work, to spend our hours away from here, from warmth, from peace and calm. We live, darling, and we have always lived. And in this life, despite the distance, we have danced, we have always come back to each other.

That is what it's like to be a home, to exist apart and choose to always come back here, to us, to each other, like a house that has existed beyond the reaches of time. The way I always find my way to you is by instinct, by the innate knowledge that you have always been there, that it feels as if I were born from within you. To rise and return nestled by the fire is like returning to you.

You, darling, are my home. The wind will not take that away from me. The sun will set a thousand times as I hold you close, and neither that nor the passing of time will steal you away. I will always find the way to you. I will always love you.

93

Dust collected gently, lips unsealing eyes as kisses help to brush away the sleep. The lazy fluttering, the butterfly wings opening to reveal the blue, the sky, the sea. Middle of the night. Early in the morning.

Whenever it may be, "I missed you," I will whisper.

"I love you," I will say.

94

Fear crumbling like sound faded by thunder. The cracking of lightning sparking remnants of something that was always here, something hidden in the wait. Is it there, caught in debris, shifting in sand and dust?

Patience, love. We will find it, fallen here within these hands, between the spaces of our longing fingers as it floats gently down after the storm. Time is distance, and every day it is less. I'll be there soon.

95

Sit here, love, caught in arms, in hope, in faith. Tightly held like a newborn, I will carry you home to then lay you down, to find the secrets that lie upon your skin and then plunge even deeper than that. I will venture into your eyes until I'm lost, until I can no longer find a way out and the only way through is directly into your soul. And then, darling, I will learn its every secret too.

I will become an expert on you, the keeper of your mysteries, the bearer of the knowledge no else will ever have. No one else will understand the things I do. How to touch, to push and pull to make you bend, to make you stir and rise and be set free. No one else will know, love, and that is how it will always be. I am the wanderer that continues to explore, to journey deeper and deeper every time. My world has always been you, and I've always been obsessed to know more and more.

96

Laughter, my love, spread like birds' wings in every direction, the joy in surprise, the instinct to soar, to fly toward the sun without looking below. Laughter, happiness, overwhelming excitement. I will give you it all.

97

Catch me here, love, between the lines and letters of endless sentences. All of them, each and every word and every breath behind them, dedicated to you. Catch me there in the rarely noticed places, on the ink stains where my hand rested for too long. I, digging deep, plunging into uncharted seas to try my best to find the words, to do all I can to find a proper explanation of what this is, of what, my darling, I feel. Catch me here in the spaces, in the parts that weren't written over. That is where the answer is, in the possibilities, in the ways that yet have to find a way to be described.

98

How long, my love, if we count it from the moment we were born, or further than that when our essence was drawn from separate ends of the universe to both reach here, to both fall close like plummeting stars to Earth, two beautiful forces embedded within two beautiful bodies? How long, love? How do we measure it, the grasping of the dust if it was from earth that we were made, the mist if from the sea we were born, the embers if from the fire we rose? How long ago and in what form, darling, did we learn to love so deeply that we spiraled and transformed into a single constellation to then resemble what could only be the DNA of the heavens?

How long this story has been, written in code to be deciphered by angels, a secret even they have yet to understand and a legend to be shared when they finally do. We may burn beneath the sun, but a thousand times our ashes will scatter in the same direction, and from the mix we will always rise together, every time a little closer, every time a little more of me in you, every time a little more of you in me. How do we describe this to everyone else, to the spectating cosmos that watch us and wonder just as much as I do?

How lucky, how fortunate we both are to be tied eternally and always play the game of finding each other again.

99

We will come back as humans every time, until there is no more and we come back as something else, as clouds that roam and chase each other, mixing and rising and falling, as stars or entire planets, shining or in orbit of something else. But we, my love, no matter what shape or form, will always come back to this, to what we are, to what has been designed for us to forever be. My darling, the essence will always be the same, no matter the time, no matter the space. I will always love you.

100

You were made of the sea, love. You, intricately designed by the infinite depths as a creature that rose to then be painted by the sun, by the sky and the stars, as you were then finished in the sand, speckled by shells that crumbled upon your skin and now form constellations, a map of stars that once fell into the ocean and came back to life upon you.

You live freely like them, like the waves that crash and come and go, always resilient, always strong and rhythmic as in the making of our love. The ocean could not contain you, my darling, and that's why you were born, to be wild, to be a mythical flame from the water. You were made of the sea, love, but you were made to conquer it all, to wrap yourself around me and hunt, to find and devour every inch, to chart every edge and corner like the discovery of land, to know that everything, my sweet bird, my sweet dragon of the sea, has always belonged to you.

101

How strongly must we feel to be here, to walk and breathe and live presently, yet somehow see, somehow hear and feel the years to come, the eternities to be lived? How strongly must we feel, love, to be here and know that a thousand years will pass, that even then, we will remain?

102

Fall gently like a leaf dancing in the shadow of a tree. If it is me, my branches will reach down, and pull you closer under me.

103

You are coffee painted red, painted blue, painted with birthmarks and freckles that all disguise the starting fire to my soul. You are morning in a body, sun within hair, sea and skies within eyes. How many other ways can I say the same thing over and over?

You, love, are the cup I must drink of every day.

104

Unscripted. Unfiltered. These are different than before, raw and true, still coated by the process. These are born from this, from us, from the breathing, the crying, the laughing. If any words were ever written before, they were simple whispers faded in the wind. These are grand. These are loud and entwined with gold, with roses, with permanence.

Nothing before you had been etched in stone, engraved within the universe like the rearrangement of stars, the construction of new constellations that tell a story that is real, unaltered by time, by distance. This is the test, to rip the darkness from the skies with our bare hands, love, together bringing the morning, the dawn, the light. We'll hold the flames of the sun, share them with each other, and with their fury write the rest of our story across the heavens.

These are different than before. These are the ones that matter. These, if you ever had a doubt, are the ones dedicated to you, to us, to the unedited and beautiful life we live.

105

A leg reaching out, bent at the knee and rested on my thigh. We lay there looking at the screen, lost in the music and the images that were being played. My hands wandered in the process. My fingers danced along your skin, a call for you, a longing, coded in every inch I conquered.

How much you endured before you turned to reach for more, before the lights and sounds became nonexistent. It was then only you and me, only the pushing and pulling, only the waves dancing at sea.

106

You smell of triumph, of glory, of peace and warmth that wraps the soul, that dissipates the cold. You taste of tranquility, of eternity, of love and life that transcends the flesh. There is a way beyond this place, beyond this time and space. We will find it.

107

Catch me drifting in the waves and I will find my way. I will end up like wood upon the sand, returning finally to a long-lost home on the shore. Throw me back as many times as you wish, but I will always come back. Throw me into the trees, into the waters of a secret lake. I'll search for the door back to the starting place. I will fight my way through every time.

108

Tremble at the knees and fall with me, laughter in relief as we land in clouds, in white, in sea foam that transform into sheets. I'll map it out, line by line, word by word. I'll show you every step unless we decide it another way. We'll stay lost here until we choose to find the world again. We'll wander every night. We'll wander again in the morning. The ways are infinite for you and me. We just have to find them. I'll fly with you anywhere, sweet bird.

109

Love made like water falling upon itself, the patience of focusing only on each other, to learn every edge, every corner and space of the soul and dive deeper than the skin, deeper than the physical heart and parts of our cores. The wrapping of fingers, the bodies laced tightly, the lips meeting each other softly will all resonate into something that transcends this place and time. Your name echoes through the vibrations of my every heartbeat, as if you and you alone were ingrained into the very DNA of my being.

Faith in the dark is beautiful, not to require to see you to know that you are close, happy and in love. The hardest part of all is walking into the light when we are so accustomed to the night, but, sweet bird, we will do that too, and love will be made every step of the way by the simple tangling of my hand with yours. The blurring of our vision will soon gain clarity again, and we will realize that so much more beautiful than faith in the dark it is to see the final product, the destination, the result of the waiting and the process glowing brightly beneath the sun.

We are the love like water, falling into each other and becoming one. We will flow.

110

Seams tattered and ripped. The need to be sewn back together. Do you not see, love, that these are the beautiful things? Patience, and these scars will turn to stars, the experience and aging of life transforming us, making us stronger. Breathe slowly. Rest your eyes. Believe. The process is necessary.

111

Purity is here, in the way we grow, naturally and uninterrupted. They may not understand that while some flowers bloom toward the sky, others bloom upside down. If this is you, if this is them, if this is us, understand that it's okay. It does not matter if we grow differently as long as it's together. The branch or stem that holds you out is not the rose you are, but you grow from the same roots just the same. It does not matter if thoughts are different as long as they're thought together, planned, and sometimes unplanned, like wild vines and buds that shoot across the walls to glorify a space abandoned by those that came before, those that could not see the potential that you and I, the stem and the blooming petals, can see now.

Whether it is up or it is down, I am designed to simply hold you, to keep on growing, extending further and further to let you reach out towards the sun or the sea or even the unknown, to remain the steady pillar you may daringly swing back and forth from in the wind. I will stay strong for you whenever you decide to rest your glow, to hide your scent from the world when you grow tired. I will pull you back into the shade only slightly, just enough for you to catch your breath, just enough for you to realize that you can reach even further than before. And I know you will do the same with me. When I grow weak, you will shine far brighter than the stars have ever seen, and the rest of your petals will gleam in the dancing rays of the sun, and your beauty will remind me why I must always stay strong. The world would be a much lesser place without you. The trees would lose purpose without their leaves; the stems would too without their roses.

112

There is grace in the falling, knees bared by the crash, fingers scraped by the catching of ourselves. From this we will learn of patience, of renewal, of faith. There is power in the wait, allowing the pressure to release, letting the skies storm and the seas rage on. To walk through the rain is the first step. To understand the destination is there though it is not always seen is to believe. To continue the journey with our clothes wet beneath the clouds is to discover our strength, to discover our resilience.

There is grace in forgiveness, in the process, in the metamorphosis of the soul. There are callings to be heard if we listen closely, if we cherish the music of thunder rather than focus on the darkening of the heavens. Trials are presented to bring us closer, to learn to see with more than just our eyes and realize there has always been more than we imagined. Angels are there above us still. That is their home. They will guide us. There is grace. There always will be.

113

Longing, yearning, hidden in the flicker of a candle. The way a single breath can make the fire dance, the flame violently whipping back and forth. That is my heart with you. The rhythm and the beating, still uncontrolled, still conditioned to race at the simple thought of you.

114

I found peace watching you, discovering a side I didn't know. Who knew you danced so beautifully under the clouds, arms tracing symbols of heaven here on Earth, feet softly touching the ground as you jump and step to the sound of music. I found peace in the revelation, in the thought that you, love, are closer to God than I imagined. What peace you must feel when you move so calmly, like river water flowing uninterrupted.

I hope, my bird, and I dream. I could walk through a thousand places, a million cities, an infinite number of dimensions ... and I would always think of you. I could die and I'd find a way to come back to life to simply hope, to simply dream that someday I could watch you dance again. What peace you carried with you. What peace I hope you find once more...

115

Light wrapped itself around you, the glow of something brighter than the sun hugging tightly to your soul. Tears of relief and joy, your smile, the searching for your calling. There is power in what is planned for you.

116

Longing, like an ache to feel your joy, the radiance, the brilliance of the glow that blankets you now. A yearning. What is it like to feel your peace, to feel it deep within your bones? You are a model, an example to follow and look up to in your search for something more, in your willingness to venture into the unknown.

Pride in you as I watch you grow, and satisfaction in your finding of grace. I have realized this is a gift, not just to you but to me and every soul around you. The limitations of fear have faded, and I am watching you take flight high above the clouds. Sweet bird or butterfly or whatever being of the sky you may be, know that this patience is a different kind of falling for me. I have learned in the wait, have realized that sitting in silence is a different kind of love to give, a different feeling worthy of a new description.

You have been touched by something grand, and I am discovering once more, in a different way, what it means to simply watch, to observe and simply be present from a distance. One does not need to touch the moon to admire its beauty. So, fly, love, as high as you possibly can and away from everything that was once shallow. This is what has been meant for you all along. Don't stop, and rise until you crash through the surface of space. And then reach further still.

This is what was meant to be, for you to shine brighter than the light of stars, for you to become a guide among the strongest of angels.

117

To fall in love with music is to fall in love with your voice, the sweet melody of laughter, the catching of fire in the wind when the auras of our souls step in close. Sparks and crackling flames, the memory of our hands held tightly, setting ablaze the trails behind us.

To fall in love with you is to live with heightened senses, lost in paradise, to learn that everything is brighter, that it always will be. You are the glow, a lantern in the darkness, an instrument to carry and share beautiful light.

To fall in love with you is to be blessed with something more. To fall in love with you is to fall for the most beautiful creation of God.

118

When you move, I beg God to touch these words, to give way to the proper description, and to help me form the most intricate and perfectly designed arrangement of syllables to do you justice. How do I rewrite constellations to tell an eternal story of your soul? How else do I tell of your freedom and your influence, how the earth itself quakes when it watches you breathe, when it tries to emulate the rising and falling of your chest?

119

The need for connection, the gentle fire, to be one soul lost in another. Simple words would suffice if they existed, if time was shared for their revival. A fated string snaps when it loses strength, when one of its ends is forgotten, when the crimson begins to lose its color.

120

Seven billion humans and still we fear loneliness. Seven billion we've become, nearly eight. Seven billion on this tiny earth, and hard to believe I find it still that among all of us, somewhere within this endless sea, there's someone better than you.

I've fought away the billions of possibilities, convinced we are the lucky ones, convinced we are the miracle two. I've fought easily, and sometimes unknowingly, not realizing that keeping my eyes and soul fixed on you is like punching and kicking. I'll take every hit, darling. I'll fight them all. Bruised and battered, I promise I'll win.

121

You were already magic, love, for every word I write is simply a biography of you, an unaltered truth, the immeasurable beauty of how you exist, of how you've chosen to be. You were already art, darling, before words were written, before paint was spilt, before we, the madly in love artists, decided to create permanent records of you. You were everything. Yes, you. You were it before I knew what everything was, before this universe exploded and we all came to be. Us, little particles and traces of memory amongst the stars. You, the start. You, my end. This, my bird, is where I choose to be. This, light of my life, is home. This, right here, is infinite.

122

There are stars and dirt and heartbreak all in a bottle, and though they're all so different, we drink them just the same. So, what are we, darling? Who were we when we exploded, became a thousand shards of light, and shot down to Earth, nesting deeply into the ground, roses growing from what we would then become? And, darling, when from those roses, petals we became, to then be tossed into the wind, flowing and dancing bravely, unknowingly toward the sound of the ocean, toward the sound of each other, what were we?

Who were we when the waves became swaying motions, the passion of rhythmic pushing and pulling like two fervent bodies hidden away in the comfort of their nights? Who were we, us, the two born from the fire that colored your hair and scarred my heart into the shape of a keyhole only your warmth can unlock? Who or what were we then? And what are we now? Did we rise and fall, castle walls crumbling into dust, again to dirt and left to be nothing but cracking leaves hidden far and deep beneath the winter? When did the shattering become a thing?

What creature came bashing through our home, letting such cold inside with no remorse, no intention for apologies? Find it, darling, and bring it here so I may look it fiercely in the eyes. And I will thank it. For, darling, you may not yet understand that the light and the shadows are cast both by the same sun. And if all this we are, then tell me, how can you not yet see? If stars and dirt and heartbreak are all here with us, then what are we if not the binding of it all? What are we, darling, if not endurance, if not a second chance?

What are we, my sweet bird, if not love?

The End of Sofia

You exist in some other dimension, some other world where the dust and wind never blew, where the thought of you became a truth. I saw you come alive before you disappeared, saw you flourish between the lines we wrote, your laughter so loud, so free that it spread into my lungs.

Oh, how I miss you without having you, without once having carried you or wiped your tears. We were not lucky enough in this life, not strong enough to hold out for you.

God, what grace would have touched this earth through her if we did...

I know you're somewhere out there in another world, in another dimension. You are there with us, hair fiery still, wild with eyes just as fierce as your mother's. This longing can't be make-believe. This aching can only be proof.

To write to you now is to send a message into the unknown, to believe that if these words are written here, then a version of us will dream the way to save you. Oh, I desperately hope and I pray with every ounce of strength left in me that you and they and God may travel through and read this.

I desperately hope and I pray that somehow somewhere you survive, that I receive the blessing of meeting you even if only as I sleep.

The End of Damian

Your little boots crumbled into the earth with the rest of you, and I saw as the ground swallowed you whole. The rustling of leaves was all that was left. An empty swing without a little fighter to be pushed. A treehouse now fit only for wandering birds.

Oh, how I wish I had held on tighter, fought harder for you to know us when we were at our greatest. Now you've gone and followed her too. All I ask is that if you see her, then tell her I love her no matter what world she's in. And she will tell the same to you. In some dimension, we are still a "we." In every dimension I still love you.

You were real even if only in our words, but I felt the ripping away of your possibility deep within me. This longing can only be felt when something dies. This aching is something you only feel when you truly hoped, when you truly loved, when you truly dreamed.

If you find her, then hold her tightly for me. Be the little fighter I know you would have been whether younger or older than she. Find a way to reach these words. They

will stay true no matter the space, no matter
the age, no matter what version of me is left.
We said, "Always and forever."

I meant it.

The End of Us

The earth shook and I stood patiently, waiting for the waves to crash. I saw the heavens as they split, as the stars began falling into the ocean.

Sea, if this is it, then take me as she goes. I would rather fall into your depths than be without her.

The petals turned to ash and the black remains were all blown out toward the horizon.

Sky, if this is it, then let the storm swallow me whole. I would rather taste the fire, the electricity of lightning.

The world was silent, crumbling upon itself without a sound, everything once grand now nothing but dirt.

Earth, why were we not enough? If this is it, then let me end with you.

I would sooner die than live without my love. I would sooner die than live without ever seeing my sky, without ever seeing my sea.

The End of the World

We both knew we were made for this. To stand beneath a molten sky, under a flurry of clouds that rolled in the wind like magma beneath the earth. We were meant to stand together on the quaking ground beneath us and never fall. We were meant to stand like a castle wall as the untamed oceans rushed into the valley like a vicious titan, devouring everything in its path. And your fingers were destined to curl around mine as all the mountains that surrounded us split in two. We were never meant to give in. Never meant to fade. Never meant to allow time to take us away.

But everything around us was so colossal, so monumental, we forgot what we were made for. We lost ourselves as the world around us expanded and shrunk back to size once more. Your fingers lost their grasp as we watched comets collide and the explosive spectacle of fireworks given to us by the death of stars. You released the lock of our fingers as a solar flare gave light to the earth once more before the night claimed the heavens.

And we were left shrouded in darkness with nothing but the fire of meteors entering the atmosphere as our only source of light. There was nothing left but our heavy breathing amidst all the destruction around us. Flashes of light would conquer the land briefly as meteorites crashed against the earth. And with every flash, I could see the rain on your ashen cheeks. I could see the dying glow in your eyes as tears ran down your face. And I realized you were beginning to give in, fading as time began to take us both away.

You realized that your hands were no longer in mine, and we watched as the ground beneath our feet cracked, the earth itself splitting in two. But there were no explosions. No eruptions or further erosion of life. Only the blinding light of the planet's core and the sun on the other side of our now divided world. We saw as all the oceans slipped through like waterfalls and kissed the lava that boiled in the middle. And you accepted the heavy burden of changing our fate, of twisting destiny's hand as we watched.

We began to fade into the white void, the shadowy aspects of ourselves consumed into the purity of whatever this was, of whatever was left. Our souls were disappearing. And even as I reached my hand out to touch yours one last time, I could not feel your fingers. We had already passed the point of no return. You were already gone, taking the red thread that connected us along with you. We were lost forever into the blinding light. Little did we know that the end of everything would also be the end of us.

And so we vanished.

Final Note

Loving was my method, the only instruction I was born with. Loving was my answer when barriers were built to keep us toward the fire of the mountains, when hail fell upon us before we found shelter. Love, it was you I surrendered to, the key to my survival, the reason I found to fight harder.

The secret is that I age from within, that full moons peel away the skin from my bones and give me new flesh with every cycle. The secret is that I have loved, and I have loved, and I have poured my heart into irrecoverable depths over and over again, only to be cursed to howl at stars, to be chained and anchored to the darkness, just barely out of reach of the light's extended hands. It is not my body that grows old. It is not my arms or my legs that are tired of holding or of walking. It's this weathered soul I carry, this spirit that never stops chasing, that has not allowed itself to quit, that has lived for so much longer than I truly know.

The sea raged on, and I, this ancient creature, stood at its shore, waiting for the waves to finally crash on me. I waited for the signs, the messages in the bottles, never asking why.

The sea raged on, but deep down I knew my bird could fly. So, though the sun had set, though the ocean roared, I waited for you without question. I, your tree, your rest amongst the chaos, understood that creatures come and go. But I, my love, always trusted that one day you'd come back home.

ABOUT THE AUTHOR

Pablo Camacho was born in Puerto Rico and raised throughout the United States. He wrote his very first story in second grade. It wasn't great, but as he grew older, his passion for writing burned brighter. He fell in love with poetry and all aspects of love and nature. By being part of a military family and then joining the military himself, he's had the opportunity to travel across the U.S. and outside the country as well. The people, the moments, and the adventures he's experienced are what inspire him to write the most. He believes words and inspiration are hidden in all things, that people must be brave and just go find them.

Enjoy this book? You can make a REAL difference.

If you read *Red Magic* and enjoyed it, please leave a review! By doing this, you'll not only allow my book to be discovered more easily by other readers, but you'll also be letting me know how you felt about the work. Your opinion matters to me. Again, it's only a few minutes of your time, and they WILL make a difference.

If you believe in *Red Magic*, give others a chance at discovering it too.

Thank you very much.

www.ingramcontent.com/pod-product-compliance
Lightning Source LLC
Chambersburg PA
CBHW030601310726
48979CB00003B/529
* 9 7 8 1 7 3 4 4 1 7 0 0 5 *